First published in Great Britain by HarperCollins *Children's Books* in 2014
HarperCollins *Children's Books* is a division of HarperCollins*Publishers* Ltd,
77-85 Fulham Palace Road, Hammersmith, London, W6 8JB.

The HarperCollins website address is: www.harpercollins.co.uk

1

Text © Hothouse Fiction Limited 2014
Illustrations © HarperCollins *Children's Books*, 2014
Illustrations by Dynamo

ISBN 978-0-00-755000-5

Printed and bound in England by Clays Ltd, St Ives plc

MIX
Paper from
responsible sources
FSC **FSC C007454**
www.fsc.org

FSC™ is a non-profit international organisation established to promote
the responsible management of the world's forests. Products carrying the
FSC label are independently certified to assure consumers that they come
from forests that are managed to meet the social, economic and
ecological needs of present and future generations,
and other controlled sources.

Find out more about HarperCollins and the environment at
www.harpercollins.co.uk/green

CHRIS BLAKE

TiME HUNTERS

STONE AGE RAMPAGE

HarperCollins *Children's Books*

Travel through time with Tom
on more

adventures!

For games, competitions and more visit:

www.time-hunters.com

CONTENTS

With special thanks to Lisa Fiedler

PROLOGUE

1500 AD, Mexico

As far as Zuma was concerned, there were only two good things about being a human sacrifice. One was the lovely black pendant the tribal elders had given her to wear. The other was the little Chihuahua dog the high priest had just placed next to her.

I've always wanted a pet, thought Zuma, as the trembling pup snuggled up close. *Though this does seem like an extreme way to get one.*

Zuma lay on an altar at the top of the Great Pyramid. In honour of the mighty Aztec rain god, Tlaloc, she'd been painted bright blue and wore a feathered headdress.

The entire village had turned out to watch the slave girl being sacrificed in exchange for plentiful rainfall and a good harvest. She could see her master strutting in the crowd below, proud to have supplied the slave for today's sacrifice. He looked a little relieved too. And Zuma couldn't blame him. As slaves went, she was a troublesome one, always trying to run away. But she couldn't help it – her greatest dream was to be free!

Zuma had spent the entire ten years of her life in slavery, and she was sick of it. She knew she should be honoured to be a sacrifice, but she had a much better plan – to escape!

"Besides," she said, frowning at her painted skin, "blue is not my colour!"

"Hush, slave!" said the high priest, Acalan, his face hidden by a jade mask. "The ceremony is about to begin." He raised his knife in the air.

"Shame I'll be missing it," said Zuma. "Tell Tlaloc I'd like to take a *rain* check." As the priest lowered the knife, she pulled up her

knees and kicked him hard in the stomach
with both feet.

"*Oof!*" The priest doubled over, clutching
his belly. The blade clattered to the floor.

Zuma rolled off the altar, dodging the
other priests, who fell over each other in their
attempts to catch her. One priest jumped into
her path, but the little Chihuahua dog sank
his teeth into the man's ankle. As the priest
howled in pain, Zuma whistled to the dog.

"Nice work, doggie!" she said. "I'm getting

out of here and you're coming with me!" She scooped him up and dashed down the steps of the pyramid.

"Grab her!" groaned the high priest from above.

Many hands reached out to catch the slave girl, but Zuma was fast and determined. She bolted towards the jungle bordering the pyramid. Charging into the cool green leaves, she ran until she could no longer hear the shouts of the crowd.

"We did it," she said to the dog. "We're free!"

As she spoke, the sky erupted in a loud rumble of thunder, making the dog yelp. "Thunder's nothing to be scared of," said Zuma.

"Don't be so sure about that!" came a deep voice above her.

Zuma looked up to see a creature with blue skin and long, sharp fangs, like a jaguar. He carried a wooden drum and wore a feathered headdress, just like Zuma's.

She knew at once who it was. "Tlaloc!" she gasped.

The rain god's bulging eyes glared down at her. "You have dishonoured me!" he bellowed. "No sacrifice has ever escaped before!"

"Really? I'm the first?" Zuma beamed

with pride, but the feeling didn't last long. Tlaloc's scowl was too scary. "I'm sorry!" she said quietly. "I just wanted to be free."

"You will *never* be free!" Tlaloc hissed. "Unless you can escape again…"

Tlaloc banged his drum, and thunder rolled through the jungle.

He pounded the drum a second time, and thick black clouds gathered high above the treetops.

"This isn't looking good," Zuma whispered. Holding the dog tightly, she closed her eyes.

On the third deafening drum roll, the jungle floor began to shake and a powerful force tugged at Zuma. She felt her whole body being swallowed up inside… the drum!

CHAPTER 1
PUP TENT

"I don't understand," said Zuma, from the back seat of the car. She looked out at the countryside whizzing past. "Where are the temples? Where are the pyramids?"

"We don't have any pyramids in England," replied Tom.

Tom's dad was driving the car in the front seat next to him. He gave Tom a curious look. "Of course there aren't any pyramids in England!" he said.

Zuma giggled as Tom's face flushed.

"Er… what I meant to say was it's *too bad* we don't have any pyramids," Tom stammered. "Because that would be really cool."

"Yes," Dad agreed. "It certainly would, especially for an archaeologist like me and a history fan like you."

"Absolutely!" Tom nodded enthusiastically. Then he sighed with relief as Dad turned back to focusing on the road. Usually he wasn't so careless when it came to talking to Zuma around other people, but sometimes he forgot he was the only one who could see or hear her.

"That was close," giggled Zuma, sliding across the car seat. Her Chihuahua dog, Chilli, stuck his head out of the open window. His pointy ears flapped in the wind.

This time, Tom remembered not to say anything back.

Having a 500-year-old slave girl for a friend could sometimes be a challenge, but Tom didn't mind. After all, it had been him who'd accidentally released Zuma from her magical imprisonment by banging a drum belonging to the Aztec rain god, Tlaloc.

And ever since then, they'd been travelling through time in search of the six gold coins that Tlaloc had scattered through history. Only by finding all six coins could Zuma win back her freedom and return to her own time.

Tom had become so used to Zuma's being there that now he barely noticed she was painted blue and wore a large feathered headdress. He had also grown very fond of her Chihuahua dog. Chilli had lots of energy, and for such a small animal he was very brave.

The car slowed down, and Tom's dad pulled over at a farm shop to pick up some supplies. When he was gone, Zuma asked, "Why are we heading so far away from home?"

"It's called going on holiday," Tom

explained. "It's something people do when they want to relax and have a good time."

"We can have a good time at your house," Zuma pointed out. "You've got that big television thingy and your computer games. And we can play tennis – I'm getting good at that."

"This is different," Tom explained. "It's called camping. We're going to spend a few days sleeping outdoors and exploring the woods."

Zuma frowned. "Why sleep outside when you've got a lovely bed?"

"Because it's fun!" replied Tom. "Don't you like roughing it?"

"I was a slave," Zuma reminded him, with a roll of her eyes. "I spent my whole life roughing it – sleeping on hard floors without even a blanket to keep me warm, waking up stiff and freezing cold. I'd much rather relax somewhere comfortable."

Dad came back with two shopping bags and put them in the back seat, right on Zuma's lap. "The campsite's just around the next bend!" he announced.

"Brilliant!" cried Tom.

"Great," grumbled Zuma.

Minutes later they were unloading the car and carrying their rucksacks and tents to a clearing beside a crystal blue lake. Chilli scurried around, barking happily, while Zuma sat on a rock, dangling her feet in the water. The shiny black pendant she wore around her neck glinted in the sun.

Tom and his dad worked together to put up the tents – a large one for Dr Sullivan and a smaller one for Tom. When Dad went back to the car to fetch the sleeping bags,

Zuma came and climbed inside Tom's tent.

"This looks a bit flimsy," she said, with a frown. "How's it going to protect us from the dangers of the forest? What happens if a giant snake tries to slither inside in the middle of the night? Or a ferocious jaguar attacks us?"

Tom laughed. "There aren't any ferocious jaguars in England," he said.

"Maybe," said Zuma. "But we can't be too careful. Let's go back to your house where it's warm and comfortable and—"

At that moment, Chilli came racing into the tent and crashed into Zuma, who fell backwards against one of the tent poles.

"Watch out!" cried Tom.

Too late. The pole went flying out of the ground, and the tent collapsed in a heap on top of them.

"Help!" cried Zuma, flailing around. "Get me out of here!"

"I'm trying!" said Tom.

Suddenly he felt hands grasping his ankles. With a firm pull, Dad dragged Tom out from under the tent. Dr Sullivan's face was as stern as one of Tlaloc's thunderclouds.

"Oops," said Tom lamely.

"Thomas Sullivan," said Dad, shaking his head. "What on earth are you playing at? Now we'll have to put that tent up all over again!"

Tom was about to explain that it wasn't his fault, but then he stopped. How could he blame it on an invisible Aztec slave girl and her dog? His dad would think he'd gone crazy!

"Sorry, Dad," he muttered.

Sheepishly, he helped his dad put the tent back up, and by then it was getting dark. As his dad prepared a camp fire, Tom went inside his tent to unroll his sleeping bag. Zuma carefully crawled in after him.

"Sorry about before," she said. "Chilli's such a clumsy thing at times. You're not going to make us sleep outside with the jaguars, are you?"

Before Tom could answer, he felt a drop

of water splash against his nose. It had started raining – *inside* the tent! Suddenly there was another figure crouching beside them. It was Tlaloc, the Aztec rain god.

His big blue body filled the cramped tent, his feathery headdress squashed against the ceiling.

"It's time for your next quest!" he roared. "And this one will be the most difficult yet! You cannot hope to succeed – you can only hope to stay alive…"

"If this is your idea of a pep talk, it isn't a very good one," said Zuma.

With a snarl, Tlaloc raised his arms and the rain suddenly stopped. Then a magical glittering mist filled the tent, whisking them away through the tunnels of time into the unknown.

CHAPTER 2

DAWN OF TIME

The magical mist cleared and Tom found himself standing at the top of a mountain overlooking a valley. The air was pure and fresh, unlike anything Tom had ever breathed before. There wasn't a person or a building or a road anywhere to be seen.

"Great view!" said Zuma. "But where are we?"

Tom looked at the bulky fur cloak draped over Zuma's shoulders. Whenever Tlaloc

sent them tumbling through time, their
clothes changed to match the style of the
period they were visiting. Tom was dressed
in a similar cloak to Zuma. Both of them
were wearing leggings made from animal
hide, and furry boots stuffed with grass.

"We're definitely a long way from home," Tom said. "I think further than we've ever been before." He pointed to the black pendant hanging around her neck. "Ask your necklace and see if it can help us."

Zuma's magical pendant gave them clues

to where Tlaloc had hidden each golden coin. Taking hold of the necklace, Zuma chanted the familiar question:

"Mirror, mirror, on a chain,
Can you help us? Please explain!
We are lost and must be told
How to find the coins of gold."

A riddle appeared on the surface of the black pendant:

Step back to the dawn of time;
To find the coin follow the rhyme.
Two men of stone – one large, one small,
You'll find a clue upon the wall.
Go down a path of bubbling blue;
When in doubt, to the right stay true;
Keep on past where the deer roam;
The brightest fire will lead you home.

"What does 'the dawn of time' mean?" Zuma asked, as the silvery words vanished into the depths of the pendant.

"If our clothes are anything to go by, I'd say we're in the prehistoric era," said Tom.

"Prehis-whatty?" laughed Zuma. "That's not a word! You're making it up."

"I'm not!" said Tom.

"What does it mean then?"

"It's a *very* old period in time," Tom explained, remembering what his dad had told him. "Way before the Ancient Romans, Greeks and Egyptians. Way before people could even read or write."

"Hmm." Zuma frowned. "So… no computer games?"

"Not really, no," said Tom.

A sudden gust of wind whipped across the mountaintop. Tom shivered, and pulled his cloak tightly around him. "Let's get down from here," he suggested. "It'll be warmer in the valley."

"Lead the way," said Zuma.

They began to pick their way down the jagged slope, careful not to slip on the loose rocks. Chilli darted ahead of them, sniffing and snuffling at the ground. The air was still cool and crisp but walking helped warm Tom up. As they carried on down the mountain, Zuma looked at her boots admiringly.

"These shoes don't look like much," she said. "But they're pretty comfortable. These prehis-whatty people couldn't have been that stupid."

"I didn't say they were stupid," said Tom. "I just said they hadn't learned to read or write yet."

"How about talking? Could they talk like us?"

"No one really knows," replied Tom. "Their words probably sounded a lot different to ours – like a lot of huffs and grunts."

"Sounds like my old master," Zuma told him. "He used to huff and grunt all the time, especially when I burned his breakfast."

Thanks to Tlaloc's magic, whenever Tom and Zuma travelled back in time they could understand whatever language the people there spoke. Even if people around here huffed and grunted, Tom would be able to understand them. He was still worried, though. This empty world felt strange and different. Whenever Tom saw prehistoric people on the TV, they were brutish cavemen who bashed people on the head with clubs and dragged them away by their hair. Had anyone even invented fire yet? Tlaloc hadn't been joking when he'd said that this would be Tom and Zuma's toughest challenge yet.

As they came down the mountain, the ground began to level out and a line of trees appeared along a ridge. Chilli barked with delight and scooted down towards the nearest tree. The dog's nose twitched excitedly as he sniffed around the gnarled roots.

"Looks like Chilli's caught a scent of something," said Tom.

"Maybe it's Tlaloc's coin," Zuma said hopefully.

"I don't think you can smell gold."

"You don't know Chilli," Zuma told him. "He can sniff out *anything*."

They followed the
Chihuahua over to the
large tree. The little dog
had stopped sniffing the
roots and was now looking
up into the leafy branches.

"You see?" Zuma said.
"The coin must be in
those branches. All we
have to do is climb up
and get it."

Tom peered into the
shadowy tree. Something

moved in the branches – but it wasn't a coin.

"Look out!" he cried.

The next moment a net dropped down from the tree, knocking Tom and Zuma off their feet and pinning them to the ground!

CHAPTER 3

TRAPPED

Tom and Zuma squirmed beneath the net, the prickly ropes scratching at their skin. Chilli had been caught in the net too, and was trying to gnaw his way free. But he was just as stuck as they were.

"It's no use," groaned Zuma. "We're trapped!"

Two shadowy figures dropped down from the tree's upper branches, landing on either side of the net. Tom cried out in surprise.

He tried to stand up, but the more he thrashed about, the more tangled up he got. The figures leaned in closer, peering at their catch through the gaps in the net. One was a grown man, the other a young boy.

A real live caveman, thought Tom. *And a caveboy!*

Like Tom and Zuma, their captors were wrapped in bulky fur cloaks over hide leggings. They wore furry brown hats made from some kind of animal skin, and carried rucksacks made from a hairy pelt. But it wasn't their clothes that made the breath catch in Tom's throat – it was their weapons. The man was carrying a bow and a quiver filled with arrows, as well as a copper axe. The boy had pulled a sharp dagger from his belt, and was pointing it threateningly at Tom and Zuma.

As they tried to wriggle free, Chilli had managed to gnaw a hole in the net big enough for his little body. Squeezing through the gap, he charged at the hunters, yapping furiously. To Tom's horror, the man drew the axe from his belt and swung it at Chilli. The Chihuahua darted out of the way, missing the blade by inches.

"No!" screamed Zuma. "Don't hurt him!"

The man jumped. "Goat talks?" he gasped, blinking in astonishment.

"Who are you calling a goat?" Zuma said indignantly.

The boy made a grumbling noise that Tom realised was a chuckle. "She's not a goat, Blood-Father," he said. "She's a girl." The boy stuck his knife back into his belt. Lifting up the net, he helped Tom and Zuma out. "Sorry," he said. "We thought you were food."

Tom and Zuma scrambled clear of the net, relieved to be free from the prickly ropes. The older hunter put away his axe. He was still scowling. "What tribe you belong?" he asked curtly.

Tom scratched his head, not sure how to answer. "My tribe isn't from around here. We've come from very far away."

"From beyond the mountains?" the hunter asked suspiciously.

"*Way* beyond them," said Zuma. At her feet Chilli was still glaring at the hunter, giving him a warning growl. Zuma picked up the Chihuahua and gave him a hug.

As the boy began to gather

the net, Tom helped him. "This is a strong net," he said, inspecting the rope. "What did you make it out of?"

"String peeled from the inside of tree bark," said the boy, beaming. "I twisted the string into a length of twine, then wove it into a net."

"Cool!" said Tom.

The older hunter gave his chest a thump and grunted. "Gam," he said, then pointed a scarred finger at the boy. "This Gam's Blood-Son, Arn."

Following the man's lead, Tom thumped his own chest and said, "Tom." He then pointed to Zuma and told the hunters her name.

"Gam glad to meet Tom and Zuma," said Gam. He let out a heavy sigh. "But still wish you were goats."

"What is it with this guy and goats?" muttered Zuma.

"Blood-Father is upset because we haven't caught any food," Arn explained. "A new tribe led by a man called Orm has come over the mountains. For months now they have been hunting on our land and stealing our food."

"Poachers," said Tom.

Gam nodded. "Orm bad man," he said. "He kills more deer and goats than he needs. Gam can't feed his tribe if enemy kills all animals for themselves."

"We aren't part of Orm's tribe, I promise," said Zuma. "And for the record, this is Chilli." She mimicked Gam, giving Chilli's chest a little thump. "Chilli not goat either. Chilli is friend."

"Why Tom and Zuma here if not

hunting?" Gam asked.

"In a way we *are* hunting," Tom explained. "We've come to find something important that's been hidden somewhere. As soon as we find it we can go home."

"Gam and Arn want to go home too," said Gam. "But because of Orm, we must travel far to hunt now."

There was a sudden noise higher up the mountain, the sound of stones crunching underfoot. Tom looked up to see a goat scrambling across the slope.

"Look, Blood-Father!" pointed Arn. "A goat! A real one this time."

"Shh," said Gam, slipping his bow from his shoulder. "Loud voice frighten goat away." Keeping his eyes trained on the goat, he pulled an arrow from his quiver and nimbly placed it against the bowstring. He took aim.

But before Gam could shoot, Tom and Zuma heard a rumbling laugh. It was Tlaloc! There was a deafening thunderclap. The goat let out a terrified bleat and bounded away, sending a shower of stones tumbling down the slope.

"No move!" Gam said urgently. "No sound! No want rockfall."

But even as Tom and Zuma froze, Tlaloc let off an even louder bang of thunder that echoed around the valley. The trickle of stones started to dislodge large rocks. The rain god had started an avalanche.

"Run!" shouted Gam.

At once the hunter began racing back towards the trees. Tom and Zuma ran after him. It was hard for them to keep up with Gam's long strides, and they were soon several paces behind. As they neared the trees, Tom realised that Arn wasn't with them. Turning around, he saw that the prehistoric boy had stopped in his tracks, and was looking up the mountain.

Tom gasped.

An enormous boulder was rolling straight towards Arn. If he didn't move fast, he was going to be squashed flat!

CHAPTER 4
CAVE DWELLERS

"Arn!" shouted Gam. "Move, Blood-Son!"

The hunter started to run back towards the boy, but he was too far away – he'd never get there in time. The boulder was picking up speed and Arn was still frozen to the spot, trembling with terror.

"Come on, Tom!" cried Zuma. "Help me!"

Tom's heart thudded as he followed the Aztec girl back into danger. Rocks were falling all around him. The air was thick with dust and loud crashes. Tom had to duck and weave to avoid the stones bouncing down the mountain. Arn's eyes were wide with terror as he stared at the boulder rolling towards him.

Zuma and Tom reached the boy at the same time; they grabbed a handful of Arn's cloak and pulled him out of the way. The three of them went tumbling to the ground, and the boulder crashed over the exact spot where Arn had been standing.

"Phew!" said Zuma. "That was close!"

"It's not over yet," said Tom, scrambling to his feet. "We need to find shelter!"

It was true. Large rocks were still bouncing down the slope. It was as though the whole mountain had come alive.

Suddenly Gam was at their side, pointing towards a dark opening in the rock face beyond the trees.

"Go there!" he shouted. "We take cover!"

Together they ran towards the cave, shielding their heads from the rain of stones and coughing in the dust. Chilli zoomed ahead of them, barking urgently. They dived inside the cave and were swallowed up by the darkness. The sound of rocks crashing down the slope was even louder now. Tom had to put his hands over his ears to drown out the din. Chilli stood at the opening of the cave, yapping at the avalanche as though it was an enemy he could fight. Zuma had to drag the little Chihuahua away to safety.

"Come here, doggie," she said. "We don't want you getting squashed, do we?"

Finally, the sound of tumbling boulders faded away. The deadly rockfall had ended. Gam kneeled down by his son anxiously.

"Arn hurt?" he asked.

"I'm fine, Blood-Father," said Arn. "Thanks to Tom and Zuma."

Gam nodded. "Thanks to Tom and Zuma," he said, patting them both on the

shoulder. A big grin lit up his craggy face.
"You save Blood-Son from big rock. Now
Gam do all he can to help you."

"Thanks," said Tom.

"Yes, thanks," said Zuma, marching back
towards the opening of the cave. "With your
help we'll be home in no time."

Arn caught her by her cape, stopping
Zuma in her tracks. "Evening will come
soon," he said. "Orm's tribe could be near
and they might capture you. Or a bear
might eat you."

"Oh." Zuma wrinkled her nose. "Well,
we don't want that, do we." She plonked
herself down on the floor of the cave. "I
guess we'll just have to stay here until
morning."

"Need fire," Gam announced. "And food."

Tom's stomach growled in agreement. He

watched as Gam reached into a small leather pouch on his belt. The hunter removed a grey lump of what looked like a dried mushroom, and a tool made from a small stone lashed to the end of a wooden handle.

Gam noticed Tom's interest and smiled. "You have flint where you come from?"

"Of course," said Tom. "It's a kind of rock, isn't it?"

Gam nodded. "Help make fire," he said. "Watch." He placed the mushroom on a mound of moss that looked like a tiny bird's nest. When he struck the grey lump with the flint Tom was amazed to see a bright shower of sparks. Within a minute the moss had caught fire, and the cave was filled with warm, crackling light.

As Arn gathered up twigs from the cave floor to toss on the fire, Gam showed Tom the other tools in his kit. They included a scraper, an awl for punching holes to help sew clothes, and even a small drill. The tools were painstakingly crafted. Tom was very impressed. Gam was nothing like he had expected. This wasn't a caveman, but a highly skilled hunter.

The cave was growing warmer. Gam removed his hat and threw off his heavy fur cloak. When he leaned over to tend the fire, Tom noticed markings on his back, like strange blue tattoos.

"What are those?" Tom whispered to Arn.

"They heal the body where it hurts," the boy explained. "We cut the skin and mark with charcoal. It helps stop pain."

"Like acupuncture!" said Tom. Of course Arn had no idea what he was talking about.

Zuma rolled her eyes. "Don't worry," she told the boy. "He's always making up funny words."

Gam reached into his rucksack and produced some flat bread and dried plums, which he and Arn shared with their guests. After nibbling some of the fruit, Chilli let out a squeaky yawn, curled up in a ball and began to snore. This made Arn laugh.

"Small beast, big snores," he observed.

The flickering fire cast a bright glow around the cave, revealing a series of pictures drawn on the far wall.

"Look at that!" said Zuma.

"Cave paintings!" Tom said excitedly. "Cool!"

They went over for a closer look. The cave paintings were simply drawn, using stick figures, but still skilful. Tom was impressed. One painting showed a line of men with bows and arrows chasing after a herd of animals. Beneath it there was another painting showing a ring of what seemed to be large standing stones.

"What are those?" Zuma asked.

"I don't know," said Tom. When he leaned in closer, his eyes lit up. "But look, there – in the centre of the circle!"

Zuma squinted at the drawing, then squealed with delight. Sure enough, floating in the centre of the ring was an image of a coin. "Tlaloc's coin!" she cried. "It has the face of the Aztec sun!"

Tom waved Arn over and pointed at the
cave painting. "What is this?" he asked.

"We call it the Ring of Stones," said Arn.
"It is a place where we worship and honour
fallen tribesmen."

"Where can we find it?" Zuma asked,
bouncing excitedly in her furry boots.

"It isn't too far," said Arn. "Close to my village." He smiled. "Come with Blood-Father and me and we will show you."

"Count us in!" said Zuma.

Across the cave, Gam let out a stern grunt. "We are glad to have friends Tom and Zuma join us," he said gravely. "But journey will not be easy. Orm's tribe prepares to attack any day now. Always chance of ambush along the way."

Tom eyed the razor-sharp edge of the copper axe glinting in Gam's belt. "We'll be safe with you," he said, smiling at the hunter. "And besides, Zuma and I have come up against plenty of dangerous warriors on our adventures. We haven't been beaten yet."

Gam nodded. "We start at sunrise," he declared. "All of us. For now, get sleep." He stretched out on the ground and closed his eyes. Arn returned to the fire and did the same. Tom suddenly realised how exhausted he was. Sleep sounded like a good plan.

But the thought of finding the fourth coin had Zuma so excited she wasn't ready for bed.

"I think I'll just explore the cave a bit," she said, heading away from the fire. She had just disappeared into the shadows when Tom heard a loud rattle.

"Zuma?" he said. "Are you OK?" He threw some of Gam's moss into the fire to make it burn more brightly. The flames shone far enough into the cave to pick out Zuma. She was crouching down, holding up a dry, white bone.

"I tripped over a pile of bones," she said, studying the one in her hand. "Looks like this used to be somebody's leg. Yuck!"

Tom looked at the bone and shuddered. "Maybe you'd better come back to the fire."

"Why?"

"It's a pile of bones, Zuma!" said Tom. "Aren't you worried how they got there?"

"Not really," replied the slave girl, tossing the bone back into the pile. "They're just bones. Back home in the Aztec capital we have giant racks filled with the skulls of human sacrifices."

"No way!" said Tom.

"If I hadn't run away, my skull would be on one of those racks too." Zuma looked around the cave, tapping her foot. "Do you know what I need? A torch, so I can look for more cave paintings. It's *much* too dark over here."

Tom was about to reply when the words

died in his throat. A light was shining behind Zuma – two lights, in fact. Two small circles. A pair of eyes. Something was hiding in the darkness.

CHAPTER 5
CAT'S EYES

Zuma gave Tom a curious look. "What's wrong?" she asked. "You look like you've seen a ghost."

"Don't. Move," whispered Tom.

His heart pounded as a giant cat padded out of the shadows behind Zuma. It was a fierce-looking creature with sharp teeth and dirty, ragged fur. At some stage it must have been in a nasty fight – there were scars across its body and it was missing an ear.

As the big cat sniffed the air, Zuma gulped and stayed very still. "Nice kitty," she murmured, a tremble in her voice. "No need to use those big old teeth on me."

Tom ignored the voice in his head telling him to run. He desperately wanted to help his friend, but how? He didn't have a weapon and he knew that any sudden movements could make the cat angry. He didn't want to give the creature any reason to attack.

His heart in his mouth, Tom watched Zuma edge away from the cat towards him. The cat watched them warily, the firelight flickering in her eyes.

"You never know," Zuma whispered hopefully. "Maybe it's pleased to see us."

The big cat threw back its head and roared, revealing two rows of sharp teeth.

"Maybe not," said Tom.

The loud roar had woken up Gam and Arn. As the big cat padded closer, the hunter rose stealthily to his feet.

"Cave lion," grunted Gam. "Tom and Zuma must be very careful."

There was a sharp yap, and Chilli bravely dashed forward to stand in front of Zuma. The little Chihuahua's teeth were bared, but the cave lion hadn't even noticed. It only had eyes for Tom and Zuma. The lion's matted tail flicked the cave floor as it stalked towards them.

Suddenly, with a roar, the lion sprang. Tom dived out of the way as a powerful paw whistled through the air where his head had been a second earlier. Hissing and spitting, the lion crouched, preparing to pounce on top of Tom. But Gam was

ready for it. Drawing back his bow, he sent
an arrow whistling across the cave, burying
itself in the big cat's paw. The lion let out

a howl of agony, and slunk back into the darkness.

"Phew," said Tom. "Thanks, Gam!"

"No need to thank Gam," the hunter replied. He went back to the fire and began to gather up his tools and clothing. "But cave lion will be back. We need to go now."

"What if we come across Orm's tribe?" asked Tom.

"We take our chances," Gam told him.

"First rockfalls, then cave lions and now enemy tribes," huffed Zuma. "There's a lot of danger in prehis-whatty times."

"No more talk," ordered Gam. "We leave."

Arn obediently scooped up Chilli and hurried out of the cave, with Gam following closely behind him. Tom had reached the mouth of the cave when he realised Zuma wasn't with him. She was staring longingly at the painting of the Ring of Stones, her gaze locked on the Aztec coin.

"Zuma!" he called, dashing back to grab her arm. "Come on!"

Just as they left the cave, they heard another blood-curdling roar booming out of the darkness. Gam was right – the giant cat hadn't finished with them. It was definitely time to go.

Outside, they scrambled over fallen rock and tall mounds of loose dirt until they reached clear ground. Then they ran as fast as they could, until the cave was far behind them. The night was cold and quiet. Tom had never seen a sky so black, with so many stars. Back home, even on moonless nights there was always a glow from the city lights.

They had all had enough of caves for one

night. Gam led them to a small wood and made camp at the bottom of a large tree. Arn, Zuma, Chilli and Tom stretched out on the ground. The last thing Tom saw before he drifted off to sleep was Gam. The hunter's eyes were wide open, and his hand rested on the handle of his axe. Tom could fall asleep safe in the knowledge that Gam would be keeping watch for them.

The next morning, Tom opened his eyes to find that Arn and Gam were already up, preparing a breakfast of fruit and bread.

"Must eat quickly," said Gam. "Long way to village."

"How do you remember your way?" asked Tom, as they trudged through the woodland. "There aren't any buildings or street signs, and the trees and rocks all look the same."

"He's right," said Zuma. "This place could do with a pyramid or two."

"We follow the rushing water," Arn said. "The water leads us home."

They came out of the woods near the bank of a wide river. The water flowed fast, pounding over rocks and churning into a swirl of white foam.

"The winter thaw has begun," Gam explained. "Snow turns to water. Water runs into river. The river becomes angry."

Keeping to the edge of the water, they hurried across the rough ground. As they came around a bend in the river, Gam suddenly stopped in his tracks.

"What is it?" asked Zuma.

Gam didn't reply. He was staring at a hilly ridge on the other side of the river.

"There," he said, pointing up at the ridge.

Tom followed the hunter's gaze. His heart thudded at what he saw. In the distance a troop of men in bulky furs like Gam's were walking in a line across the ridge. There must have been nearly fifty of them. Each carried at least one weapon; some had two or three – axes, bows, blades – all of them deadly-looking.

"Are they friends of yours?" Zuma asked hopefully.

Arn shook his head. "It's Orm," he said. The young boy looked angry. "He is leading a hunting party into our lands again."

"Worse than that," grunted Gam. "Too many men for just a hunting party, Blood-Son. All of Orm's warriors. We must go."

"Where?" asked Tom.

"Our village is on the other side of that ridge," Gam replied. "Orm has brought all of his warriors to attack it. They will take our food and burn our huts to the ground. We have to warn my tribe."

"But how?" said Tom. "They're miles ahead of us!"

"We go by river," said Gam.

"You want us to *swim*?" said Zuma, her eyes wide. "You must be joking!"

Tom had to agree. The river was bursting with icy, melted snow, and thundering down through the rocks. They wouldn't last a minute in the freezing water.

"Swim?" Arn laughed. "No. We have a better idea."

He and Gam moved over to some large stones beside the river's edge. As Tom looked closer he saw that someone had placed a woven grass mat over a gap between the stones, covering something beneath. His eyes widened as Gam and Arn dragged out a wooden canoe from between the rocks. Then the hunters dragged out a second canoe.

"We store these here to use when the water is calmer," Arn explained. "Usually we wouldn't use them when the river is flowing this fast, but we have no choice. We have to warn our tribe before Orm attacks them!"

As they positioned the canoes on the
edge of the bank, Tom looked out over the
raging water, trying not to look nervous.
One mistake in the canoe, and they would be
carried away on the current and smashed into
the jagged rocks poking out of the water.

Still, there was no time to be scared. Gam had saved Tom and Zuma from the cave lion. Now it was up to them to help him warn his tribe.

He took a deep breath and stepped into the first canoe, taking a seat at the front of the craft. Behind him Gam rolled up the woven grass mat and placed it in the bottom of the second canoe.

"Zuma, you will come in this canoe with me," he told her. "Blood-Son Arn will travel with Tom. We know the river. You will be safe with us."

But before Arn could get in Tom's canoe, a wave of freezing spray came up from the river, drenching the bank. Chilli howled and sprang backwards, knocking into Zuma and sending the pair of them tumbling over.

"Look out!" cried Tom.

With a squeal Zuma landed in Tom's canoe, knocking it off the edge of the bank and sending it crashing into the water!

CHAPTER 6

WILD WATER

The canoe flew down the river, carried
away on the foaming white water. Zuma
had fallen on her back, while Chilli had
buried himself in the bottom of the canoe.
Dazed, Zuma pulled herself up and took the
seat behind Tom.

"I hope you know how to steer this
thing!" she yelled, over the rushing water.

Tom didn't have a clue. It was the first
time he'd ever been in a canoe. But if he

didn't learn fast, they would be torn apart on the rocks in the river. Picking up a wooden paddle, he plunged it into the water and paddled for his life.

"Come on!" he called out to Zuma. "Help me!"

Zuma found her paddle and began pulling it through the water. Together they struggled to keep the canoe upright. Spray was flying up from the river, stinging their eyes. On the bank behind them, Tom could see Gam and Arn hurriedly pushing their canoe into the water and paddling after them.

"Look out!" cried Zuma. "Rock!"

A spiky rock loomed up in front of them. Digging his paddle into the churning water, Tom frantically tried to steer the canoe around it. Together he and Zuma fought against the current, which seemed determined to hurl them into the rock. There was a loud groaning sound as the canoe grazed the side of the rock, and then it slipped past.

There was no time to celebrate – the

canoe was still hurtling down the river. Working together, Tom and Zuma managed to keep the craft steady, even as it bounced and tossed in the powerful current. Within a few minutes Arn and Gam caught up with them, setting the two canoes on a side-by-side course. "You're doing fine!" Arn called.

Now that he had got the hang of canoeing, Tom felt exhilarated by their journey along the wild river. Zuma giggled as the craft rose over the waves and crashed down again, sending up an icy spray. Chilli was the only one of them who wasn't having fun. He bolted from one side to the other in a panic.

"Don't get too close to the edge, Chilli," Zuma warned. "The water's getting even rougher up ahead." But the Chihuahua was already standing on his hind legs with his front paws on the front of the canoe, barking at the waves.

Zuma was right – Tom could feel the current growing stronger. He had to work even harder to keep his oar steady when he dipped it into the water.

They came to a sharp bend in the river, and when their canoe went whipping around it, Tom could see enormous rocks jutting out of the water like broken teeth. Here the current was like lightning, moving even faster and harder as it swirled around the jagged stones.

The next moment, the canoe nearly tipped over, bouncing off a rock with a jolt. The craft lifted out of the water, hitting the surface again with a *smack* that sent Chilli flying over the side and into the foam.

"Chilli!" screamed Zuma.

Tom held his breath until the dog surfaced, sputtering and swimming for all he was worth in the freezing froth.

"We have to save him!" Zuma cried.

Paddling as fast as they could, Tom and Zuma steered the canoe towards Chilli. The little dog's head was bobbing on the surface as he tried to keep afloat. The canoe wobbled as it pulled closer, threatening to throw them all overboard. Leaning over the side, Zuma reached out and plucked her dog from the river by the scruff of his neck.

"Chilli!" she sighed, cuddling the sopping wet dog in her arms. "Thank goodness."

But in the rush to rescue Chilli, the canoe had veered down a narrow channel leading off the river. Gam and Arn had been taken by surprise, and were continuing away down the main part of the river. Arn turned in his canoe and shouted something, but Tom couldn't hear him over the roar of the water. There was no way they could turn the canoe – the current was just too strong. They would have to carry on down the channel and hope for the best.

"I have no idea where we're going," said Tom.

"Maybe it's a shortcut to Gam's village," Zuma said hopefully.

A shiver of anticipation ran down Tom's spine. The sooner they got to the village, the sooner they could warn Gam's tribe. But Orm's men were marching ever closer. If Tom and Zuma weren't careful, they would be caught up in the middle of a dangerous battle – and without Gam to protect them. Still, they couldn't turn back now. They couldn't let their new friends down.

"Fork," Zuma said suddenly.

Tom blinked with surprise. "What?" he said.

"*Fork!*"

"Come off it, Zuma!" Tom scolded. "I'm hungry too, but this is no time to be thinking about food!"

"No! I mean there's a fork in the river!"

Tom felt his stomach sink. Ahead of them the river split, cutting itself in two. And without Gam and Arn to guide them, they had no way of knowing which route to take.

"Left or right?" asked Zuma, her paddle poised.

Tom had no idea. Then his eye caught the black pendant around Zuma's neck, glistening with water droplets. It reminded him of the riddle: *Go down a path of bubbling blue; when in doubt to the right stay true…*

"Right! We need to go right!" he shouted.

Together they began paddling furiously towards the right branch of the river. They had to fight the current, which seemed determined to drag them to the left. Tom's arms were soon aching from the effort. Behind him Zuma gritted her teeth and dug deeper into the water with her paddle. Chilli barked in encouragement.

It was then they heard a thundering sound. Tom's first thought was that Tlaloc was nearby, ready to cause trouble again.

But this wasn't just a single thunderclap
– this was an endless crashing roar. Tom
looked towards the left branch of the
river and saw that it ended in a towering
waterfall.

Zuma gulped. "Uh-oh!"

"Faster!" cried Tom. "Paddle faster, or we're done for!"

They redoubled their efforts and at the last second the canoe pulled clear, rocketing down the right-hand branch of the river and away from the waterfall. The water was pouring down the waterfall on to a jagged row of rocks below. If the canoe had gone over it, it would have been smashed to pieces – along with Tom and Zuma!

CHAPTER 7
ON THE HUNT

As they left the waterfall behind, the water grew calmer. Tom and Zuma's canoe drifted gently along, and they saw that they were going to rejoin the main river. When they did, they heard a splashing sound behind them. Tom turned to see Gam and Arn paddling up to their canoe. Both the hunter and his blood-son had been looking worried, but they smiled with relief when they saw Tom and Zuma were unhurt.

"Gam fear you were dead," said Gam. "Worried the water ate you."

"Ha!" Zuma gave a dismissive wave. "It's going to take more than a few bumps in a river to beat us."

"We saw you go off down the channel, but we couldn't follow you," Arn told them. "It took a lot of skill to come out alive. How did you manage to avoid the waterfall?"

"Well," grinned Tom, with a glance at the black pendant hanging around Zuma's neck. "Let's just say we had a little help."

"Head for the riverbank," Gam instructed. "We go ashore here."

Obediently, Tom and Zuma paddled towards the river's edge, where there was a thick wood. The canoe had barely brushed against the bank when Chilli threw himself on to the grass and rolled around joyfully.

He was obviously very happy to be back on dry land!

As Gam dragged the canoes on to the bank, his face darkened.

"What is it, Blood–Father?" asked Arn.

Gam pointed to the ground. "Fresh tracks," he said. "A large group of men walked through here not long ago."

Tom's heart sank. After all they had been through on the river, they still hadn't managed to overtake Orm's warrior party. There was no time to waste. They plunged into the trees, not waiting to cover up the canoes with the woven grass mat.

Inside the wood it was dark and cool. As they walked quickly along a narrow trail, they heard animals scampering through the leafy undergrowth. High above their heads, birds called out to one another in strange screeches and chilling shrieks. Tom shuddered when he felt something slither across his feet. Everywhere he looked in the shadows, he thought he saw one of Orm's men, ready to jump out.

"I think I'd rather be back dodging rocks on the river," he whispered to Zuma.

"Me too," Zuma whispered back.

The narrow trail curved to the left. As they marched on, Tom saw a bush on the edge of the path shake violently.

"Look out!" he cried. "There's someone in there!"

"Get back!" Gam ordered. He drew his bow and nocked an arrow on the string.

The bush rustled again, and a large deer sprang out on to the path. Tom had never seen such an imposing animal before. It was a stag, with a large rack of antlers above its head. The startled deer took one frightened look at the humans and went bounding off along the path. Gam pulled back on the string and let the arrow fly, expertly bringing down his quarry with one shot.

"Well done, Blood-Father!" Arn called out. "Now we can feed the village!"

"We're going to take the deer with us?" asked Tom.

Gam shook his head. "No time," he said. "Leave deer here. Come back for it later."

They hid the deer's body beneath a pile of branches and carried on along the trail. Gam and Arn fell silent, and Tom could tell that they were worried about their tribe.

The trail led to a clearing in the middle of the wood. Sunlight poured in through the gap in the trees, melting the shadows away. Chilli dashed across, making straight for a tangled shrub on the far side of the clearing.

"Don't go too far, Chilli!" Zuma told him. "We haven't got time to go looking for you if you get lost!"

The little Chihuahua sniffed excitedly

around the base of the shrub. He barked.
The leaves began to quiver and shake.

"What have you found there?" said
Zuma. "Is it another deer?"

With a bloodcurdling roar, a burly
warrior charged out of the undergrowth, his
axe blade glinting in the light. Tom's blood
froze. It was one of Orm's
men! The warrior ran
past Chilli, making
straight for Zuma.
She yelled with
fright, and ducked
as he swung his
axe. The blade
made a deadly
whistle as it sliced
through thin air.

Gam let out a

furious bellow and drew his axe. With a
wicked smile, the warrior turned away from
Zuma and ran towards the hunter. There
was a loud ring as their weapons clashed.

"Run, Blood-Son!" Gam roared to Arn.
"Warn our village!"

He quickly brought up his axe, blocking
a thrust from the other warrior just in time.
The two men snarled at each other, each
trying to push the other back. Arn looked
like he wanted to step in and help, but Tom
pulled him away.

"Listen to your Blood-Father," he shouted.
"We have to try and save your village!"

Chilli barked in agreement, and scurried
out of the clearing. When Tom and Zuma
ran after him Arn reluctantly followed,
leaving Gam still wrestling with Orm's
tribesman.

They raced through the wood as fast as they could, jumping over roots and ducking beneath low branches. Tom ran until his lungs burned, determined not to be the first one to stop. Beside him Zuma's face was red, but she showed no sign of slowing down.

Finally, the wood came to an end. When they emerged from the trees on to a grassy plain, Zuma's face went pale. "Look," she said, pointing at the sky. "Smoke."

Just beyond a nearby hill, clouds of thick black smoke were rising into the air.

"Our village is burning," cried Arn. "We're too late!"

CHAPTER 8
TRIAL BY FIRE

They raced up the hill towards the village. Even before they could see it, Tom could smell the smoke and hear the sounds of battle – blades crashing, arrows whistling, axes thudding. The air echoed with shouts.

Gam's village was a small collection of wooden huts on top of the hill. Smoke was rising up into the sky from where some of the roofs had caught fire. Men were fighting with axes and clubs in and out of the huts.

In the thick of the battle a giant figure in a wolf-skin cloak was swinging a wooden mace with a stone head.

"Orm," said Arn, through clenched teeth. "We have to stop him."

"How?" asked Tom. "We don't have any weapons!"

Gam's tribe had been caught off guard by the surprise attack. As Orm's warriors pressed forward they fell back into a circle. They seemed to be taking orders from a grey-haired man waving a giant axe.

"Who's that?" asked Tom.

"His name is Col," Arn replied. "He is a noble warrior and our tribe elder, the most important man in our village. My Blood-Father has great respect for him."

A sharp bark from Chilli made Tom whirl around. One of Orm's warriors had

crept up the hill behind them, a dagger in
his hand. The man lunged forward at Tom,
who just managed to twist out of the way.
The surprised tribesman carried on charging
past him and Zuma stuck out her foot. The
warrior tripped over it and fell sprawling to
the floor.

"Thanks, Zuma," panted Tom. "We've got to get some weapons or get out of here. This is really dangerous!"

Arn was already racing up the hill towards the village. Tom and Zuma had no choice but to go after him. The air was black from the smoke coming off the burning huts. Luckily the fighters were so busy battling with each other that they didn't notice Tom and Zuma slipping past them. They spotted Arn taking cover behind one of the thatched huts. He had picked up a bow from the ground and was firing arrows at the invaders.

"What are you doing?" asked Zuma.

"This is my home," Arn said proudly. "I must defend it, just like Blood-Father!"

At that moment the defenders let out a ragged cheer. Tom's heart thumped with relief as he saw Gam charging up the hillside towards the village. The hunter had survived his one-to-one combat in the wood. Now he yelled a war cry at the top of his lungs, swinging his axe in a deadly arc as he fought his way over to the rest of his tribe.

"Blood-Father!" Arn cried joyously. "He will save the village!"

Gam stood shoulder to shoulder with the tribe elder Col, and together the two of them began to push back Orm's men. Arn stepped out to fire his bow once more, only to duck as a flaming arrow flew over his head and buried itself in the roof of his hut. Within seconds the roof was alive with crackling flames.

"Our hut!" cried Arn.

Above the sound of the fighting, Tom heard Gam cry out. He turned and saw that Col had fallen to the ground, an arrow sticking out of his chest. The elder was dead.

"Help us, Blood-Father!" Arn cried out to Gam. "Our home is burning!"

Hearing his son's cry for help, Gam left the fallen elder and fought his way through the battle until he reached Arn. The entire wall of their hut had gone up in flames. Tom, Zuma, Arn and Gam had no choice but to back away from the blaze.

"There must be something we can do!" said Zuma.

Tom was deep in thought. Without a weapon, he couldn't help fight off the invaders. But maybe he could think of a way to stop the village from burning to the ground.

"We can fill buckets at river," said Gam. "Bring them back to pour on flames."

From the way those flames were jumping, Tom knew that buckets would take far too long. He pictured the firemen he'd seen in TV news stories, battling enormous blazes with giant hoses and endless supplies of water. What he wouldn't give to have a fire hose right now.

But maybe he had the next best thing.

Throwing back his head, Tom yelled at the sky, "Hey, Tlaloc! Where are you, you big sissy?"

Zuma looked at him in shock. "Have you gone crazy!?" she yelled. "Things are bad enough without bringing Tlaloc here. You're going to make him angry!"

"I know!" Tom hissed. "That's the whole point!"

"Oh, *I* get it," she said, smiling. Then, cupping her hands together, she shouted out:

"Tlaloc! Come out, come out, wherever you are! Call yourself a rain god? *Pain* god, more like!"

"You big chicken!" Tom shouted, for good measure. "We're not frightened of you!"

A roll of thunder hammered through the sky. It was so fierce and loud that the battling tribesmen paused in their fighting to look upwards. They saw a rolling mass of black clouds appear out of nowhere to blot out the sun. But it was only Tom and Zuma who saw Tlaloc's furious blue face scowling down from the stormy sky.

"You DARE to insult me?" Tlaloc roared, over another rumble of thunder.

"Insult you?" Zuma shouted back. "We haven't even *started* yet. Drain god!"

"Vain god!" added Tom.

Lightning bolts of pure rage shot out from Tlaloc's eyes, arrowing down from the sky and striking the ground in the heart of Gam's village. The tribesmen scurried for cover, all thoughts of fighting gone for the moment.

"Missed us!" Zuma jeered. "Not even close!"

Tom laughed. "Why don't you show us what you can *really* do?"

Tlaloc narrowed his eyes. Tom held his breath. *I hope this works*, he thought. As the tribesmen stared in amazement, Tom raised his arms in a mighty, god-like gesture.

Splat! A fat raindrop hit the dry ground right beside Tom's foot. Then the storm clouds exploded, sending sheets of rain down from the sky and soaking everything in sight.

"Yes!" cried Zuma.

The heavy downpour instantly put out

the burning huts, leaving them sizzling and smouldering but still standing. Orm's tribe huddled around their leader, staring at Tom in awe.

"The boy summons storms!" said one, pointing at Tom.

"So?" barked Orm. "He is no match for Orm, the mighty warrior!"

Zuma rolled up her sleeves and stepped forward. "If I were you, I'd get off this land and never come back," she warned. "Or I'll bring on something much worse than a silly little rainstorm."

"*Silly little rainstorm?*" Tlaloc seethed. The storm clouds bubbled, and then there was another clap of thunder. It was so loud that the huts of Gam's village shook. Tom's ears rang. Orm's tribe was looking at Zuma in shock.

"*Both* of the small ones can control the sky!" howled one of them. "Run for your lives!"

The rival tribe turned and fled down the hill away from the village. Orm tried to stop them but his men ignored him. Abandoned and outnumbered, the humiliated chief had no choice but to follow.

"And don't come back!" Zuma called after him. Chilli barked in agreement.

"Something tells me he won't," laughed Tom.

Zuma winked up at Tlaloc, whose blue face was still frowning down from the sky. "Sorry about that," she said breezily. "It was just a joke. A little time-travel humour."

"Not funny!" Tlaloc snarled.

"It was my fault, not Zuma's," said Tom. "I'm really sorry."

"Don't *ever* try and play tricks on me again," the god warned. "Or I'll chase you with lightning bolts to the ends of the earth!"

Tlaloc disappeared in a swirl of grey cloud, taking the rain with him. The sky was once again clear and blue. Gam's tribe shuffled around Zuma and Tom. They were staring at them with open awe.

"Gam's friends can use the weather like a weapon!" said one.

"They are gods!" exclaimed another.

"Not really," said Tom. He was feeling anything but god-like. Even through his heavy furs he was soaked to the skin. When he turned to Zuma, he saw that her hair was wet and straggly and her face was covered in soot. Even so the villagers were still looking at them with a mixture of gratitude and fear.

"Tom and Zuma saved us," said Gam, his

voice filled with respect. "How can we repay you?"

"Can you take us to the Ring of Stones?" asked Zuma.

Gam nodded, his face sober. "Tomorrow, first light. The whole tribe will make journey to sacred Ring of Stones."

"Why the whole tribe?" asked Tom.

Gam looked over to where Col lay on the ground. "Our tribe elder is dead," he said solemnly. "We will bury him there."

CHAPTER 9
THE BRIGHTEST FIRE

Just before dawn a hand shook Tom awake. For a moment he thought it was his dad, waking him for an early morning hike or a dip in the lake. Then he opened his eyes and saw Arn, and everything came back to him. He wasn't at a cosy campsite. He was thousands of years away, somewhere in the prehistoric mountains. And if he and Zuma couldn't find Tlaloc's coin, they were going to be stuck here. Forever.

"Rise and shine, lazybones," said Zuma, over Arn's shoulder.

The Aztec slave girl had already got up, and was feeding Chilli a scrap of meat. Tom sat up and stretched. From outside he could hear 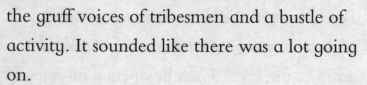 the gruff voices of tribesmen and a bustle of activity. It sounded like there was a lot going on.

"It is nearly time to go to the Ring of Stones," Arn told Tom. "There we will help you finish your hunt."

"Where's Gam?" asked Zuma.

Arn beamed with pride. "Blood-Father is very busy," he told them. "He has been made the new tribe elder. He will make sure our village is safe and that our people have food to eat from now on."

Tom smiled. "I know he will, Arn."

When they left the hut, Tom saw tribesmen starting to mend their charred homes. A man with curly brown hair seemed to be in charge, pointing people this way and that.

"That's Pag," whispered Arn. "He is the best builder in the tribe. He will make sure that the new huts are strong and do not fall down."

A lot of huts had been damaged by fire during the battle. Pag was going to have his work cut out. He looked happy enough, though, as he ordered some young tribesmen to go and bring him back some wood.

One of the huts had managed to come

through the battle without a scratch. When Tom looked through the open door he saw people chopping up meat in front of a roaring fire in the hearth.

"After you went to bed," Arn explained, "I led a hunting party back for the deer Blood-Father had killed." Arn explained. "Orm's tribe were so scared they must have run straight past it. We will have a great feast today – thanks to you."

A feast sounded like a good idea to Tom. He was starving. But eating could wait. First they had to find Tlaloc's coin.

In the distance they saw a procession slowly leaving the village. As the new tribe elder, Gam was at the front. He was dragging a wooden sledge with Col's body on it. The hunter's face was solemn. Tom, Zuma and Arn joined the back of the procession and followed it away from the village. No one spoke. Even Chilli didn't let out a single yap.

As they walked through the grassy countryside the sun began to rise, casting a pale light over a large hill rising up before them. At the top of the hill there was a ring of standing stones. The hairs on the back of Tom's neck stood up as he climbed. He had been on a school trip to Stonehenge once, but this was different. At Stonehenge he could see cars moving along the nearby road. But this Ring of Stones was in the middle of a vast, empty land. No birds flew over it. No animals could be seen around it. There was a strange, magical atmosphere about the place that made Tom's skin tingle.

Tom had a thousand questions to ask Arn about the stones, but he knew it wasn't the

time. As the procession entered the ring he saw that a grave had been dug in the ground in the middle. Gam dragged the sledge over to the grave and gently laid Col's body in the earth.

The sun had lifted itself a bit higher beyond the mountains, bathing the Ring of Stones in yellow light. Tom and Zuma stood silently as the mourning tribesmen stepped forward and laid Col's weapons and valuables in the grave beside his body.

"I hope none of those treasures is Tlaloc's gold coin," Tom whispered to Zuma. "Otherwise we'll never get it back."

When the tribesmen had finished, Gam took care of the sad task of burying the body. Then he and Arn came over to join Tom and Zuma.

"These stones symbolise the heroes who live in our legends," Arn explained. "Most are named in honour of our gods." He smiled. "And now two of them will bear the names Tom and Zuma."

Zuma blushed.

"Wow, thanks," said Tom. "That's a great honour."

Chilli let out a disappointed whine, and Arn laughed. He picked up a small rock and placed it beside the stone called Zuma. "This one can be called Chilli," he said.

Chilli wagged his tail in delight.

They were now the only people left in the Ring of Stones. With Col buried, the rest of Gam's tribe were heading back down the hillside and returning to their village. Tom and Zuma exchanged a glum expression.

"What's wrong?" asked Arn.

"We still haven't found what we are looking for," Tom explained. "We think there's a gold coin hidden somewhere here, and we need to find it."

"Can you help us look for it?" Zuma asked. "Please?"

Tom, Zuma, Gam and Arn spread out, searching all around the circle. Even Chilli joined the hunt, burrowing at the base of the tallest stone, which had recently been named Tom. But no coin was found in the dirt or anywhere else.

"It's not here!" said Zuma. She threw up her arms in frustration.

At that moment the sun rose fully above the hills. A single shaft of brilliant light shot out across the Ring of Stones. Tom blinked. At the top of Zuma's stone, something was glinting in the light. Shading his eyes against the glare, Tom looked closer.

There, at the top of the stone, embedded in the rock itself, was the golden coin — complete with the face of the Aztec sun etched into it — smiling down at them.

"We've found it!" cried Zuma. "But how are we going to reach it?"

"I have an idea," said Tom.

He asked Gam to give him the scraper from his belt. Then he climbed up on to the hunter's shoulders. Reaching up with the scraper, Tom was able to prise the coin out of the rock.

Clutching the coin triumphantly, Tom jumped down from his perch.

"You did it!" cried Zuma, lifting Chilli from the ground and touching the coin. At once the magical mist rose up to surround them.

"Thanks, Gam and Arn!" called Tom. "Good luck rebuilding your village!"

"More magic!" breathed Gam. "You *are* a god!"

They were the last prehistoric words Tom heard before they once again entered the tunnels of time and travelled back to the present day.

CHAPTER 10
HAPPY CAMPING

Tom, Zuma and Chilli landed on Tom's sleeping bag with a soft thump. They were back inside his tent. Outside Tom could hear a fire crackling. His dad was whistling as he made dinner. Whenever they returned from the past, time had stood still.

But time wasn't the only thing that waited for them… Tlaloc was also right where they'd left him, crouching in the tiny tent in the middle of a heavy indoor

rainstorm. The Aztec god looked furious, his bulging eyes even bigger than usual.

"We did it!" said Zuma, plucking the coin from Tom's hand and flipping it to Tlaloc. "Coin number four, and it's all yours."

Tlaloc's face darkened. "You deceived me," he growled at Tom, pointing a gnarled finger at him. "You tricked me into sending a storm to help you."

"We didn't have a choice," said Tom. "It was the only way to save Gam's village. We did what we had to do."

"Then so will I," Tlaloc said ominously. "The next quest will be truly impossible. You will pay for mocking me!"

"Bring it on," retorted Zuma. "Whatever you throw at us, Tom and I can take it."

The god shot her a final wicked look, then raised his arms and vanished in a loud thunderclap.

"Tom?" came Dr Sullivan's voice from outside the tent. "You must have finished laying out your sleeping bag by now! Dinner's ready."

Tom scrambled out of the tent to find his dad sitting at the edge of a camp fire, cooking sausages on sticks over the flames. Tom thought back to Gam's fire in the cave, and the meal of bread and dried fruit they had shared together. Perhaps things hadn't changed all that much in five thousand years.

As he looked at the browning sausages Tom's stomach rumbled loudly. They'd left the Stone Age before the village feast, and he was really hungry. He sat down next to his dad and eagerly took one of the sticks. When the sausage was cooked he took a

bite. It was delicious! He wolfed down one, and then another.

"Someone's hungry," said Dad, his eyes twinkling merrily.

"You have no idea," Tom laughed. "I feel like I haven't eaten in an age!"

"A *stone* age," added Zuma. The invisible Aztec girl was lying on the grass on the other side of the fire from Tom, warming her feet by the flames. Chilli barked happily and nestled into her lap. Zuma giggled, and gazed up into the starry sky.

"Maybe you were right," she told Tom. "After our trip to the Stone Age, I think I can understand why you were so excited about camping. Roughing it *can* be fun."

Tom looked around at the camping gear that he and his father had brought with them. They had lanterns and flashlights, waterproof tents and warm sleeping bags. Then he thought of Gam's little pouch of tools – the flint striker and the scraper, the awl and the small drill. What would the Stone Age hunter make of all this hi-tech equipment?

He finished eating and pushed his plate to one side.

"Still got room for some pudding?" asked Dad.

Tom nodded.

Dad smiled and produced a bag of marshmallows from behind his back. Tom's eyes lit up.

"This is the best camping trip ever," he declared.

Dad fanned the fire to coax up a flame, then watched as Tom happily stuck two plump marshmallows on to a stick. He held the sweets over the fire to let them warm up.

"How did you manage to work up such a big appetite?" his dad asked. "All we've done so far is put up the tents."

And outrun an avalanche, survive a raging river, and save a burning village, thought Tom.

"I guess it's all the fresh air that's making me hungry," he fibbed. He looked across at Zuma to give her a knowing grin, only to find that she and Chilli were already sound

asleep beside the fire!

Popping one of the gooey, sweet
marshmallows into his mouth, Tom smiled.
He had no idea what Tlaloc might have in

store for him and Zuma on their next trip through time, but he did know one thing for certain.

He couldn't wait to find out.

TURN THE PAGE TO . . .

➤ Meet the REAL Stone Age men!

➤ Find out fantastic FACTS!

➤ Battle with your GAMING CARDS!

➤ And MUCH MORE!

WHO WERE THE MIGHTIEST STONE AGE MEN?

Because Stone Age man lived in a time before people could read or write, it's hard to be sure exactly who he was or how he lived. We've based our characters on what historical facts we *do* know about the Stone Age...

GAM is a Stone Age hunter who leads Tom and Zuma into battle against a rival tribe. By the Stone Age, hunters had learned to make tools to catch and kill animals to eat. The frozen remains of one Stone Age hunter, whom archaeologists call Ötzi the Iceman, show he had an axe, a dagger, a bow and arrow, a backpack and a net. He must have been strong!

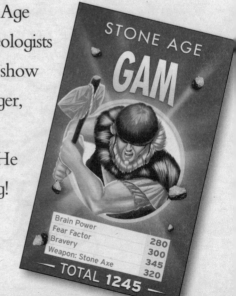

STONE AGE

GAM

Brain Power	280
Fear Factor	300
Bravery	345
Weapon: Stone Axe	320

— TOTAL **1245** —

COL is the elder of Gam's tribe and was once a mighty warrior. We know from digging up Stone Age skeletons that there were lots of battles in this period. The bow and arrow were invented around 12,000–10,000 BC, and

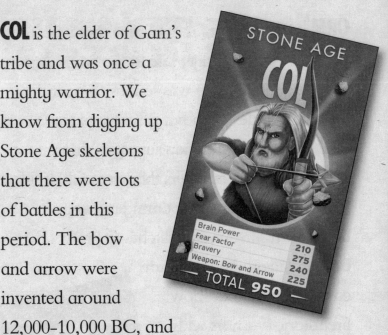

STONE AGE

COL

Brain Power	210
Fear Factor	275
Bravery	240
Weapon: Bow and Arrow	225
TOTAL	**950**

graves from around 7000 BC have been found containing weapons such as daggers, slings and maces. Judging by the remains of warriors archaeologists have found with broken skulls and arrowheads in their bones, Stone Age battles were pretty brutal.

ORM is the leader of a rival tribe that wants to conquer Gam's village. Life in the Stone Age was tough, and there was serious competition for food. Battles often happened at places where there was a steady supply of things to eat, for example by rivers that were full of fish. The first forts were built during prehistoric times, with surrounding ditches to protect them from invaders. And there are cave paintings that show prehistoric warriors with bows and arrows hunting in a straight line – the very first battle tactics!

STONE AGE

ORM

Brain Power	250
Fear Factor	320
Bravery	280
Weapon: Mace	300

TOTAL 1150

PAG is a builder and a member of Gam's tribe. By the Stone Age people no longer lived in caves. In fact many of them lived in wooden houses built on stone foundations, with a hearth inside for fires to keep them warm. Pag would have

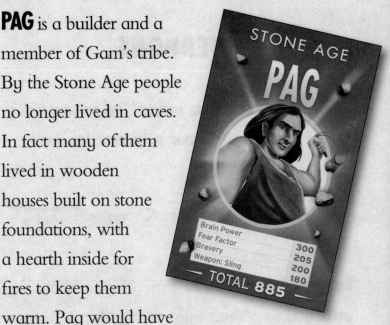

also made sure that the village was built on top of a hill, to make it harder for rival tribes like Orm's to attack it. Stone Age people didn't just build houses. They also constructed rings of large standing stones, where they would bury people and worship their gods. Perhaps the most famous example of this is Stonehenge in the United Kingdom.

WEAPONS

Stone Age men were fierce warriors! Find out what kind of weapons were used in the Stone Age.

Tanged Spearhead: a metal spearhead attached to a shaft by a prong, dating from the early Bronze Age (2500–1500 BC).

Flint Knife: a piece of flint that was carved into the shape of a blade and mounted on a wooden hilt.

Flint Arrowhead: a slice of flint chiselled into a point and attached to a wooden arrow.

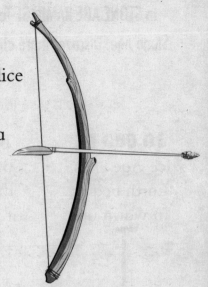

Polished Stone Hand Axe: a crudely smoothed-down stone attached to a shaft, and wielded as an axe.

STONE AGE TIMELINE

In STONE AGE RAMPAGE Tom and Zuma go back to the Stone Age. Discover more about it in this brilliant timeline!

6500 BC
Rising seas cut Britain off from Europe, turning it into an island.

10,000 BC
Ice Age ends. Earth begins to warm up.

5000 BC
Invention of the wheel.

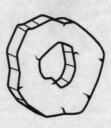

8000 BC
Last of the Ice Age animals such as the woolly rhinoceros and the sabre-tooth cat become extinct.

4500 BC
Stone and flint begin to be mined.

3100 BC
First ditches dug at Stonehenge.

3350 BC
Death of Ötzi the Iceman, one of the most famous prehistoric remains.

3000 BC
Beginning of the Bronze Age.

TIME HUNTERS TIMELINE

Tom and Zuma never know where in history they'll travel to next! Check out in what order their adventures actually happen.

10,000 BC–3000 BC
The Stone Age

AD 1427–AD 1521
The Aztec Empire

AD 1185–AD 1868
Feudal Japan

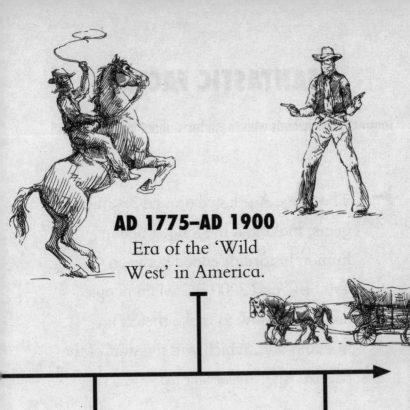

AD 1775–AD 1900
Era of the 'Wild West' in America.

AD 1492–AD 1607
First contact between Native American tribes and European settlers in America.

AD 1850–AD 1880
Bushranger outlaws become famous in Australia.

FANTASTIC FACTS

Impress your friends with these facts about the Stone Age!

→ The Stone Age lasted around 3.4 million years, making it the longest age in human history! It ended between 4500 BC and 2000 BC when people discovered how to make metals by smelting ores, which was the start of the Bronze Age. *About time too!*

→ During the late Stone Age – or Neolithic Age – carpentry really took off. Small branches of trees were woven into fences and the walls of round houses. They were then wind-proofed with a mixture of straw, clay and animal dung. *Gross!*

➤ It took over a thousand years (between 4500 BC and 3500 BC) for British people to go from travelling hunter-gatherers like the Stone Age men to farmers with established communities. *That's a long time to be wandering around!*

➤ 'Henges' or ritual stone rings like Stonehenge or Avebury in Wiltshire started to appear between 3300 BC–1200 and are only found in Britain and Ireland. *Rock on!*

➤ Because Stone Age men didn't have a properly formed language, they used gestures to communicate, and cave paintings to tell stories. *Cool!*

WHO IS THE MIGHTIEST?

Collect the Gaming Cards and play!

Battle with a friend to find out which historical hero is the mightiest of them all!

Players: 2
Number of Cards: 4+ each

➜ Players start with an equal number of cards. Decide which player goes first.

➜ Player 1: choose a category from your first card (Brain Power, Fear Factor, Bravery or Weapon), and read out the score.

➜ Player 2: read out the stat from the same category on your first card.

➜ The player with the highest score wins the round, takes their opponent's card and puts it at the back of their own pack.

➜ The winning player then chooses a category from the next card and play continues.

➜ The game continues until one player has won all the cards. The last card played wins the title 'Mightiest hero of them all!'

STONE AGE

GAM

Brain Power	
Fear Factor	
Bravery	280
	300
Weapon: Stone Axe	345
	320
— TOTAL **1245** —	

For more fantastic games go to:
www.time-hunters.com

BATTLE THE MIGHTIEST!

Collect a new set of mighty warriors – free in every
Time Hunters book! Have you got them all?

COWBOYS

- [ ] Wyatt Earp
- [ ] Wild Bill Hickok
- [ ] Buffalo Bill
- [ ] Billy the Kid

COWBOYS
WYATT EARP
Brain Power
Fear Factor
Bravery 300
Weapon: Bullwhip 285
320
TOTAL 1235 330

SAMURAIS

- [ ] Lord Kenshin
- [ ] Honda Tadakatsu
- [ ] Lord Shingen
- [ ] Hattori Hanzo

SAMURAI
LORD KENSHIN
Brain Power
Fear Factor
Bravery 320
Weapon: Katana Sword 280
320
TOTAL 1260 340

OUTBACK OUTLAWS

- [ ] Ben Hall
- [ ] Captain Thunderbolt
- [ ] Frank Gardiner
- [ ] Ned Kelly

OUTBACK
BEN HALL
Brain Power
Fear Factor
Bravery 290
Weapon: Bushranger Knife 300
380
TOTAL 1250 280

STONE AGE MEN

- [ ] Gam
- [ ] Col
- [ ] Orm
- [ ] Pag

BRAVES

- [ ] Shabash
- [ ] Crazy Horse
- [ ] Geronimo
- [ ] Sitting Bull

AZTECS

- [ ] Ahuizotl
- [ ] Zuma
- [ ] Tlaloc
- [ ] Moctezuma II

MORE MIGHTY WARRIORS!

Don't forget to collect these warriors from
Tom's first adventure!

GLADIATORS

- [ ] Hilarus
- [ ] Spartacus
- [ ] Flamma
- [ ] Emperor Commodus

GLADIATORS
HILARUS

Brain Power
Fear Factor   180
Brainer   250
Weapon: Gladius   330
                     165
TOTAL **925**

KNIGHTS

- [ ] King Arthur
- [ ] Galahad
- [ ] Lancelot
- [ ] Gawain

KNIGHTS
KING ARTHUR

Brain Power
Fear Factor   340
Bravery   390
Weapon: Broadsword   270
                     400
TOTAL **1400**

VIKINGS

- [ ] Erik the Red
- [ ] Harald Bluetooth
- [ ] Ivar the Boneless
- [ ] Canute the Great

VIKINGS
ERIK the RED

Brain Power
Fear Factor   305
Bravery   235
Weapon: Axe   260
                     310
TOTAL **1110**

GREEKS

- [ ] Hector
- [ ] Ajax
- [ ] Achilles
- [ ] Odysseus

PIRATES

- [ ] Blackbeard
- [ ] Captain Kidd
- [ ] Henry Morgan
- [ ] Calico Jack

EGYPTIANS

- [ ] Anubis
- [ ] King Tut
- [ ] Isis
- [ ] Tom

GREEKS
HECTOR

Brain Power	295
Fear Factor	320
Bravery	340
Weapon: Sword	300
TOTAL	**1255**

PIRATES
BLACKBEARD

Brain Power	300
Fear Factor	270
Bravery	345
Weapon: Cutlass	400
TOTAL	**1315**

EGYPTIANS
ANUBIS

Brain Power	350
Fear Factor	400
Bravery	360
Weapon: Fear	400
TOTAL	**1510**

CHRIS BLAKE

TIME HUNTERS

FREE GAMING CARDS INSIDE

MOHICAN BRAVE
Battle the mightiest!

Who were the Braves?
How did they live?
What weapons did they fight with?

Join Tom and Zuma on another action-packed
Time Hunters adventure!

They landed with a bump in a wood. When
the mist cleared, the autumn air was fresh
and crisp, with a pleasant earthy smell. Tom
looked around and saw that the trees blazed
with colour. The leaves were different shades

of red, orange and gold. The undergrowth was thick with green ferns, and in the distance Tom caught sight of a sparkling blue river.

"Wow! It's so pretty," Zuma said in a hushed voice. "Where do you think we are?"

Tom hoped what they were wearing would give them a clue. Zuma was no longer painted blue and feathered. Her dark hair was now twisted into two long plaits. The black necklace was the only thing that remained of her Aztec clothing. Both she and Tom were dressed in soft leather breeches and tunic-style shirts. Leather fringes dangled from their sleeves and the front was decorated with beaded patterns. On their feet they wore beaded leather moccasins. Tom had seen similar ones in the North American section at his father's museum.

"We're dressed like Native Americans,"

he said. "But North America is a really big continent so I'm not sure exactly where we are."

Zuma hugged her arms around her and shivered. "Brr!" she said. "It's certainly colder than where I come from. The sooner we find that coin the better!"

"Then let's see what your pendant has to say," Tom suggested.

Zuma took the black disc in her hand and held it up to the light to recite the familiar incantation:

"*Mirror, mirror, on a chain.*
Can you help us? Please explain!
We are lost and must be told
How to find the coins of gold."

There was a shimmer of silver across the gleaming stone as words rose to the surface:

On the banks of the water

You'll find a sun, then seek a daughter.
With the bravest of braves you'll use your wiles
To find the pretty stream that smiles.
Weather's mysteries you shall know;
You'll shiver with your quiver in an early snow.
But October storms are soon to melt;
The treasure lies within a belt.

Zuma sighed. "Why can't it ever just say, 'the coin is hidden under the third tree on the right'?"

Tom was about to reply that it wouldn't be much of a riddle if it did, but before he could open his mouth, Chilli caught the scent of something. The dog let out an excited bark and dashed deeper into the woods.

"Let's go!" cried Zuma, taking off after him.

Tom followed, kicking up dried leaves as he ran. Chilli was in hot pursuit of a small brown and white rabbit. The rabbit disappeared down a hole and Chilli would have followed if Zuma hadn't reached out and caught him.

"Where are you going, silly?" she asked. "We need you to help us find the coin."

As he tried to catch his breath, Tom caught a glimpse of gold glittering between some bushes. *Could it be the coin?* he wondered. Tlaloc never usually made their tasks so easy. He grabbed Zuma's sleeve and pointed.

Then from out of the undergrowth, a creature stepped forward, two shining gold eyes staring out from its face.

"Hello, little doggie!" cried Zuma in delight.

Chilli began to wag his tail and wriggle in Zuma's arms.

"Chilli wants to make friends," said Zuma.

The creature swished its bushy orange tail.

Zuma was about to set Chilli back down on the ground, but Tom stopped her just in time.

"That's not a dog," Tom said. "It's a fox." He patted Chilli on the head. "Better keep your distance, boy. Foxes can be dangerous. Their teeth and claws are very sharp."

Chilli let out a whimper of disappointment and they carried on exploring the forest. Aside from the rustling of leaves and the chirping of birds, the woods were silent. There didn't seem to be any paths, and there was no sign of a town or city anywhere.

"I wonder if we're the only people here," Tom said aloud.

An odd warbling noise suddenly echoed through the woods. Moments later, a flock of birds trotted into view. Dark feathers fanned out from their backs, and lumpy red skin dangled from their necks.

Zuma hid behind Tom and shuddered. "Ugh!" she said. "Are those hideous creatures dangerous too?"

Tom laughed. "No," he said. "Turkeys won't hurt you, they just look strange."

"I think you mean *ugly*," said Zuma. Suddenly, her eyes went wide and she pointed. "Duck!" she cried, pulling on his arm.

"Not duck, *turkey*," Tom corrected her.

"No… *duck*!" Zuma dropped to the ground, just as an arrow came whizzing over her head.

Too late, Tom understood what she was saying. He whirled round in the direction the arrow had come from and saw a flash of feathers sticking out from behind a tree. Then he heard a *thwang* and a *whoosh*…

Another arrow flew through the air and

tore through his shoulder.

"Owwwww!" Tom howled in pain.

He looked at his arm. The sleeve of his buckskin shirt had torn and blood was trickling out of a gash.

"Tom!" cried Zuma, pulling him to the ground. "Are you OK?"

Tom nodded and tried not to let out another moan. "I don't think it's too deep," he said through gritted teeth.

"I guess that answers your question," Zuma said, as another arrow whizzed past them. They caught a flash of bright feathers sticking out from behind a tree trunk.

"What do you mean?" Tom asked.

"We definitely aren't the only people around!" Zuma said. "And whoever else is here doesn't seem very happy about having company!"

A dark-haired figure dressed in buckskins stepped out from behind the tree, his bow poised, an arrow already held against the taut string.

And it was pointed directly at Tom's heart.

★

"Please don't shoot!" said Tom, hoping that the stranger would understand him. That's how Tlaloc's magic had always worked in the past. But with an arrow aimed straight at his chest, he couldn't take anything for granted. Tom put his hands in the air to show the stranger he meant no harm.

As the stranger came closer, Tom could see that he was only a boy, not much older than they were. He wore brilliantly beaded buckskins and his cheeks were smeared with swirls of yellow and red paint. Like Zuma, his long hair had been wound into two glossy plaits. Around his forehead was a beaded band with two bright crimson feathers sticking out of it.

"I like your paint and feathers," Zuma remarked in her friendliest voice. "Have you ever thought of trying a bit of blue? It's not a bad look."

The boy blinked at her, confused.

"It's probably not the time to give him fashion advice," Tom whispered, "when he's got an arrow pointed at my chest."

As if remembering what he was doing, the boy quickly lowered the weapon. Tom heaved a sigh of relief.

"I'm so sorry!" said the boy. "I didn't mean to hurt you. I thought you were a deer." He gave them an embarrassed grin. "Actually, I hoped you were."

"Don't worry," said Tom, clutching his wounded arm. "Accidents happen."

The boy bent down to examine Tom's wound. "It's not too bad," he said. "But it's still bleeding." He crouched beside the roots of a tall tree and gathered up a handful of green moss.

"This is no time for gardening," huffed Zuma.

The boy laughed. "This isn't gardening, it's medicine." A dark look passed over his face as something had just occurred to him. "You're not Mohawk, are you?"

"I'm an Aztec," said Zuma.

"And I'm British," said Tom.

The boy thought it over, then shrugged. "I do not know either of those tribes. But as long as you're not Mohawk, I am happy to help you."

Tom watched as the boy pressed the clump of fuzzy green moss to his cut. In seconds, the moss soaked up the blood.

"That's clever," said Tom.

"Yes," said the boy, crossing to a young willow tree and peeling off some strips of bark. "And this willow bark will make a good healing tonic once I take it home and boil it up. Do you feel well enough to walk to my village? It's not far, just round the bend there."

"Village?" said Zuma, sounding relieved. "So there are other people here?"

The boy nodded and helped Tom to his feet. "Yes. My people are called the Mohican." He started walking towards the water. Tom and Zuma followed.

"My name is Rising Sun," the boy said. "What are you called?"

Tom replied for both of them. "I'm Tom,

and this is Zuma."

Chilli let out an indignant bark.

"And this is Chilli," added Zuma, giving
the dog a pat.

As they travelled through the woods, Tom
noticed how silently Rising Sun moved,
avoiding things like fallen twigs. Tom copied
him, trying to walk as quietly as he could.

"We call ourselves Mohican," Rising Sun
explained, "because it means 'People of the
waters that are never still'."

Tom eyed the swift current churning under
the surface of the wide blue river. It sparkled
in the autumn sunlight. "I can see why," he
said.

"Why were you worried that we might be
members of the Mohawk tribe?" Zuma asked.

Rising Sun scowled. "Because they are
enemies of the Mohicans. They live on the

other side of the river. And they are trying to drive us away so they can have these hunting grounds for themselves."

"That doesn't sound very fair," said Zuma.

"Is that why you're wearing war paint?" Tom asked excitedly. "Because you're going into battle with the Mohawk?"

Rising Sun touched the squiggles he'd painted on his cheeks and forehead. "We believe these symbols and colours have magical powers." He smiled sheepishly. "And I need all the help I can get."

"What do you mean?" asked Tom.

"I'm a terrible hunter," the boy admitted, looking embarrassed. He nodded towards Tom's shoulder. "I mistook you for a deer."

Zuma gave a wave of her hand. "It could happen to anyone."

"That's the problem," sighed Rising Sun.

"I'm not just anyone. I'm the son of Chief Tall Oak. My father is our tribe's leader and also our greatest hunter and warrior. So of course I'm expected to be like him."

"Maybe all you need is a little practice," Tom suggested.

"But I don't want to be either of those things," Rising Sun explained. "What I really want is to be a medicine man. I like caring for others, and I'm good at healing injuries."

"My, er, tribe calls that being a doctor," said Tom. "And doctors are very important and highly respected."

"Why can't you just tell your dad you'd rather be a medicine man?" asked Zuma.

Rising Sun shook his head sadly. "The son of a powerful chief is expected to be a brave warrior. That's why I was sent out here alone today – to test my hunting skills and prove my bravery. But as you can see, I haven't done very well. I'm going home empty-handed."

"No, you're not," said Zuma, scooping Chilli into her arms. "You've got us! And we're much more interesting than a smelly old deer!" She giggled, but her joke failed to cheer up Rising Sun.

"My father won't be proud of me," the boy said darkly. "A hunter has to feed his family, and a warrior must be able to fight skilfully. I can't do either." He pointed ahead, to a cluster of small, round huts. "Here is my village."

"Great!" said Zuma. "I'm freezing. Do you think there'll be a fire where I can warm up?"

"Of course," said Rising Sun. "My people are very friendly and welcoming."

The words were no sooner out of his mouth when Tom heard Zuma gasp. Three huge Mohican braves stepped soundlessly into their path, blocking their way.

Tom turned to go back the way they had come, but found himself staring up at three more Mohican braves who had appeared silently behind them. These warriors were as frightening as the first three. All six wore feathered headbands and held sharp weapons, poised to strike.

Tom looked up into their painted faces and tried to remember what Rising Sun had said about his tribe being friendly and welcoming. Because as the braves glared down at him, Tom wasn't feeling very welcome at all!

THE HUNT CONTINUES...

Travel through time with Tom and Zuma as they battle the
mightiest warriors of the past. Will they find all six coins
and win Zuma's freedom? Find out in:

Got it! ☐

Got it! ☐

Got it! ☐

Got it!

☐

Got it!

☐

Got it!

☐

Tick off the books as you collect them!

DISCOVER A NEW
TIME HUNTERS QUEST!

Tom's first adventure was with an Ancient Egyptian mummy called Isis. Can Tom and Isis track down the six hidden amulets scattered through history? Find out in:

Got it!

Got it!

Got it!

Got it! ☐

Got it! ☐

Got it! ☐

Tick off the books as you collect them!

Go to:

www.time-hunters.com

Travel through time and join the hunt for the
mightiest heroes and villains of history to win
brilliant prizes!

For more adventures, awesome card
games, competitions and thrilling news,
scan this QR code★:

★If you have a smartphone you can download a free QR code reader from your app store.